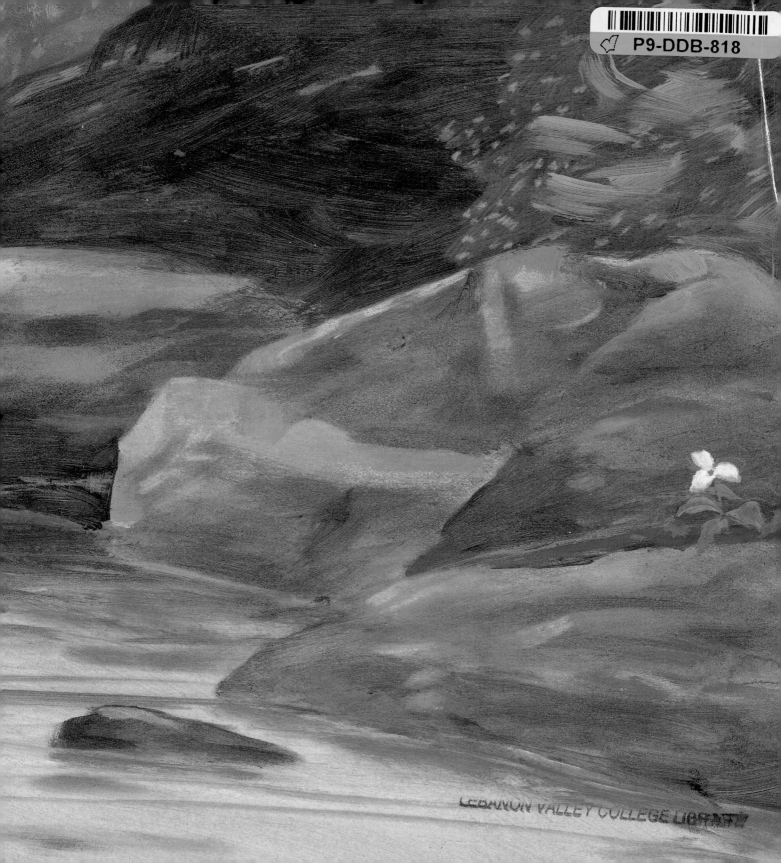

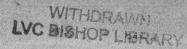
Angel Coming

written by Heather Henson

illustrated by Susan Gaber

Atheneum Books for Young Readers

New York   London   Toronto   Sydney

For Daniel, my own precious bundle
—H. H.

For Mary B. and Adeline C.,
and with thanks to Jason Flahardy
—S. G.

Mama says an angel is coming,
coming clear up the mountain,
riding clear up Lonesome Creek,
a tiny babe tucked in her saddlebag,
a tiny babe tucked safe and warm.

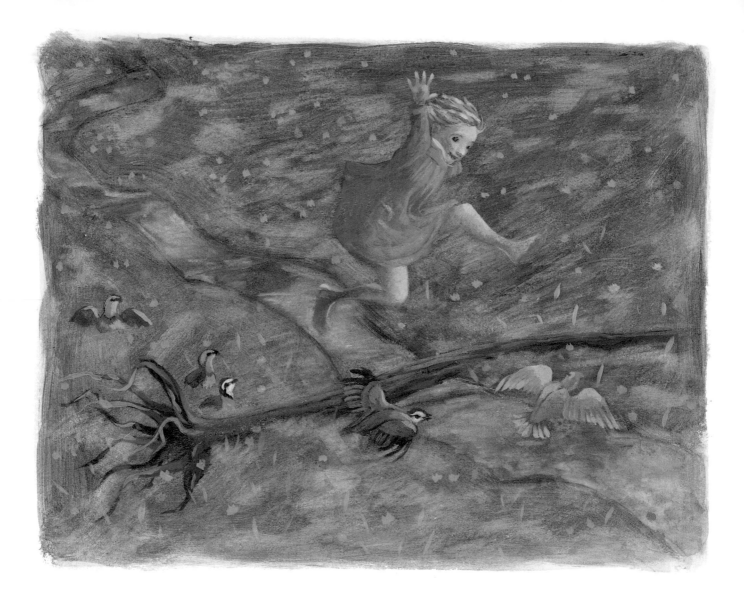

Mornings now I take to running,

running to look-see down the hill

where the creek talks soft and low,

where the bobwhites dart and call—
my own special place for catching
an angel on a big black mare.

Mama says we must be ready,

ready for that angel coming.

So Pap brings down the cradle

carved out smooth from cherry wood,

whittled pretty with vines and roses,

made for me when I was new.

Then we wash the bitty clothes—
bitty caps and gowns and britches—
hang them in the bright day sun.
Mama says I was the first to wear them,
but I can't figure I was ever that small.

Saturday the aunties come a-calling,

calling with a quilt to stitch.

All day long they sit and chin-wag.

All day long they make it grow—
Tree of Life with names upon it,
branches reaching wide and strong.

Aunties say our folks have been here,
been here 'bout a hundred year.
Aunties tell the old-time stories,
and they keep the old-time ways.
They watch for signs and see a fortune
stirring in a cup of tea.

Soon a blue moon starts to rising,
rising up old Bobcat Ridge.
That's when Pap takes down his banjo,
picking quick as summer lightning,
tunes to get a body moving—
clapping hands and stomping feet.

"Boy or girl?" Pap does the asking,

asking once the folks have left us,

and the night is quiet still.

Mama says there's none can reckon—

not even the aunties with their knowing—

only that angel coming up the mountain.

Me I think I know for certain,

certain as my blue moon wish.

Li'l sis is what I'm wanting.

Li'l sis is what I'll call her.

I'll braid her hair right pretty,

brush it out most every night.

Morning comes with fog to tuck us,

tuck us in like her very own babes.

Times like this the cows stay close,

and the hens keep to the gilly trees.

A troublesome day for catching angels,

'cause ears hear more than eyes can see.

So in the mist I am a tracker,

tracker from old times gone.

Up the mountain path I follow

panthers, bears, and wolves a-prowling.

Higher still I'm queen and ruler—

I'm higher than the sky does sit.

Hoot owl hoots and I go racing,

racing shadows back down the hill.

Home again I find a lady

standing near a big black mare.

Tall as Pap and wearing britches,

saddlebag across one shoulder,

nothing in it I can tell.

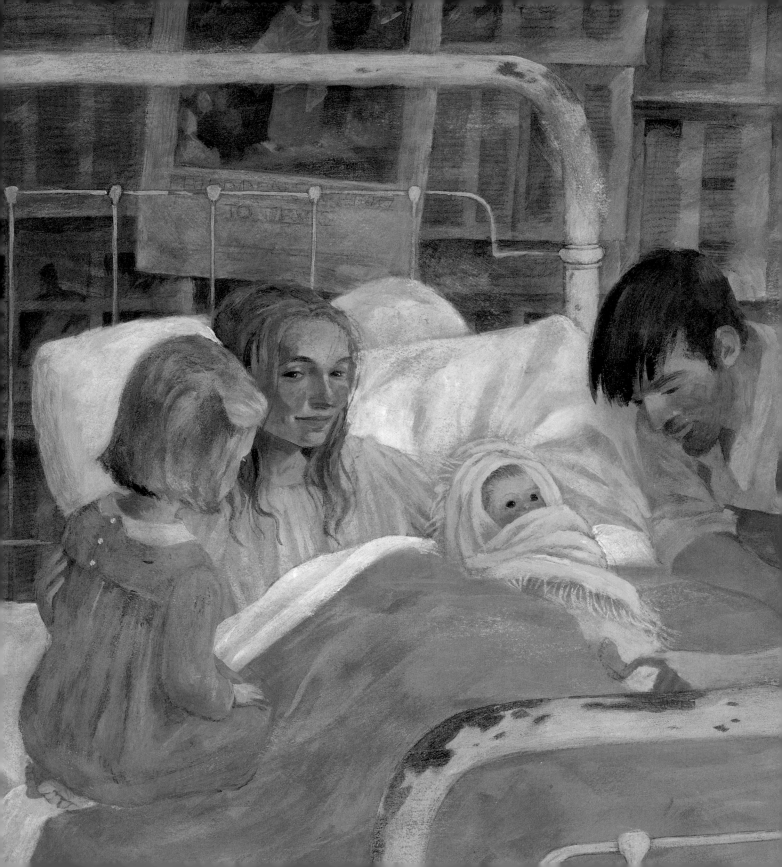

I hurry quick to find my mama,

Mama with a joyful face.

Rosy babe right close beside her—

bitty fingers and bitty toes,

but eyes as big as teacup saucers,

watching all the world to see.

To think I almost missed that angel,

angel coming clear up the mountain,

bringing us this precious bundle.

Li'l brother is what I'll call him,

not the sister I had wished for. . . .

Can't help but love him just the same.

Author's Note

Not so long ago in the Appalachian mountains of Kentucky, if a child asked where babies came from, the reply given was utterly unique. Folks would tell of babies brought up the steep paths, tucked safely inside saddlebags, carried by an angel on horseback.

Of course this notion is as likely as the stork or a baby found in a cabbage patch, but as often happens with folklore, a kernel of truth exists: the angel was real.

In 1925 Mary Breckinridge created the Frontier Nursing Service in Eastern Kentucky, the first of its kind in America. Mary was from an aristocratic southern family, but instead of choosing a life of leisure, she became a nurse because she wanted to help others. She chose Kentucky because she knew from having spent time there as a girl that medical care was desperately needed.

Going up into the mountains of Kentucky in the 1920s was like stepping back in time. Many families lived in log cabins without electricity or running water. There were no telephones or radios or cars. Roads were just creek beds or paths cut into the steep terrain. Folks traveled by foot, horse, or mule.

Few doctors ventured into this remote region. Diseases like diphtheria and typhoid fever were ravaging the hillsides, and complicated births were leaving families motherless. Mary knew that women and children in particular were dying at an astonishing rate here, and she was determined to do something about it.

And so she built a clinic and advertised for nurse-midwives who wanted adventure and were not afraid of hard work—and that's exactly what she got. At first the proud mountain people did not know what to think of these strong-willed young women in their smart blue uniforms, but in time they came to trust and depend upon these "angels on horseback."

As part of her job each "angel" had her own "route" or section of the mountain, and she would make monthly visits to check on a family—weekly visits if a mother was soon expecting a child. Sometimes, as in this story, a routine visit might happily coincide with the blessed event.

The Frontier Nursing Service is not simply a part of history—it continues the dream Mary Breckinridge began so many years ago. Today there is a hospital and a school to train whole new generations of nurse-midwives. And there are jeeps now instead of horses for house calls. High in the mountains of Kentucky, however, the spirit of the angel on horseback lives on.

A photograph taken by Mary Breckinridge's cousin
during the 1930s to show the bit of mountain
folklore: how babies were brought in saddlebags

The women of the Frontier Nursing Service

Mary Breckinridge

The author and illustrator wish to
thank the Frontier Nursing Service
for their help and the use of
the photos on this page.

Atheneum Books for Young Readers • An imprint of Simon & Schuster Children's Publishing Division • 1230 Avenue of the Americas, New York, New York 10020 •
Text copyright © 2005 by Heather Henson • Illustrations copyright © 2005 by Susan Gaber • All rights reserved, including the right of reproduction in whole or in
part in any form. • Book design by Kristin Smith • The text for this book is set in Old Claude. • The illustrations for this book are rendered in acrylic paint. • Manufactured
in China • First Edition • 10 9 8 7 6 5 4 3 2 1 • Library of Congress Cataloging-in-Publication Data • Henson, Heather. • Angel coming / Heather Henson ; illustrated
by Susan Gaber.—1st ed. • p.   cm. • Summary: A family makes preparations, eagerly awaiting the arrival of the angel who will come up the mountain bringing a new
baby. • ISBN 0-689-85531-1 • [1. Mountain life—Fiction. 2. Babies—Fiction.] I. Gaber, Susan, ill. II. Title. • PZ7.H39863Ang 2005 • [E]—dc22   2003027981